Deadly Night Shades

Ken Smart was the new rookie on the beat on Isla Verdante. Big City wasn't equal to it's name, but it was an average medium-sized town type of place for the Caribbean Islands.

Capt. "Handy" O'Connel seemed to take an instant dislike to Ken. He didn't know why.

Ken's father had been a good cop, in the states. Chicago. Twenty five years. He had retired, and had died a year later. Ken always thought he had willed himself to die. He didn't feel he had a purpose anymore. Ken had learned to love/hate the career, but was deter-mined to keep up the family tradition. His grandfather was a cop.

Ken got assigned to the graveyard shift. He would prove his mettle or get bounced.

He was determined. All he needed was some kind of anchor for his determination.

He found it the second night on duty: a killer who had been around for sixteen years. He killed every six months. Ken found his thirty fourth victim.

Could he find this killer?

Contents

About the author

CD Moulton has traveled extensively over much of the world both in the music business, where he was a rock guitarist, songwriter and arranger and in an import/export business. He has been everything from a bar owner to auto salvage (junkyard) manager, longshoreman to high steel worker, orchid grower to landscaper, tropical fish farmer to commercial fisherman. He started writing books in 1983 and has published more than 350 books as of January 1, 2023. His most popular books to date are about research with orchids, though much of his science fiction and fantasy work has proven popular. He wrote the CD Grimes, PI series, and the Det. Nick Storie series, Clint Faraday series, and many other works.

He now resides in Gualaca, Chiriqui, Panamá, where he writes books, plays music with friends, does research with orchids and medicinal plants. He has lately become involved in fighting for the rights of the indigenous people, who are among his closest friends, and in fighting the extreme corruption in the courts and police in Panamá.

He offers the free e-book, *Fading Paradise*, that explains what he has been through because of the corruption.

CD is the discoverer of the Chadam Protocol for curing cancer.

Facebook page Ambrosia peruviana for cancer.

Deadly Night Shades

<u>*New Cop*</u>

Kenneth Arnold Smart, 22, from Chicago, just finished police academy (though he knew the trade well. His father and grandfather were cops in Chi), and finding a job in Big City (which it wasn't), Isla Verdante, Caribbean Sea, ran his fingers through his lush brown hair as he stepped off the 707, and looked over the town from his position at the top of the landing platform. He had never been in a place like this. It was as beautiful as the pictures. He'd thought it would be hot, here in the tropics, but there was a breeze that made it comfortable.

He checked his bags through, and got a decrepit cab to take him to Wellwright Hotel, where he would be housed for the first month, if he was accepted. He had applied for a job from an ad in the Gazette, and was amazed that he got it.

He did have excellent grades, in the academy. The ad said a cop from the Chi area would have extra consideration. Apparently, he was the only one from there who applied.

The hotel was better than he expected. He was used to an old walk-up, so this seemed almost luxurious. He had a balcony that looked over a fantastic blue-green sea. There were a couple of sailboats, just offshore, and a sleek yacht was going by, a little farther out.

This was on the line between Upper Big City, where the rich and semi-famous spent time, and the residents were definitely upper-end. Two blocks away was Lower Big City. There were two marinas, right across the line from each other. Million dollar (and more) yachts and sailboats on "his" side and outboards and beat-up older boats on "their" side. Ken noted that there were only whites here, except for a number of the hotel workers. They were mostly blacks and Latinos on the other side.

He was used to that, in Chi. The real trouble came from the lower side, in Chi, and probably here. Maybe the way the town was set up was why they wanted a Chi cop.

Most big cities had that kind of thing. Upper crust and slums not far apart. Here, the line was more pronounced than Chi. Tenth Street was the line. The people, he would later learn, called it "Divider Road." The "uptown" and "downtown" sections weren't a matter of elevation.

Ken always got along with people. In his mind, there was no division. They were all individuals. The so-called "Upper Crust" had as many thieves and criminal types as the lower. They weren't so publicized, and seemed to concentrate in other areas. The violences were, to a great extent, much more in the poorer sections. That was too often brought on by desperation and frustration.

The poor here seemed to live a better life than in Chi. There were no tin sheds or tarp tents, here. Not in the city. The houses seemed solid and well-kept, to a great degree.

He had noted people on the taxi ride to the hotel. The airport was, of course, just past the lower city. God forbid that those noisy jets come over *my* house at all hours.

There were two jets per day. 9:30 and 4:30. There were a number of the smaller "Island Hoppers" that used the airport. There were no lights, and no night flights.

There were some mean-looking customers on the streets, in the lower end. What they called a "threatening stance" in Chi. Big Rastas, and what would be the pimps and dealers, at home. Fancy clothes, expensive jewelry, gold chains. He was told that wasn't the case so much, here. It was for status among their own peer group.

They looked violent, but generally weren't a violent people, though that was changing as the city grew. It always did. Drugs weren't a big problem in the lower end, though there was a lot of cocaine available. They worked against that, but ganja was mostly ignored. The whites were the main users of the coke, though they bought it from the blacks. The Latinos were more or less neutral, in that area. The word was that blacks sold it, whites used it.

There was a lot of random noise, in the form of loud music. The people seemed happy, and danced to it, spontaneously, at times. It was mostly calypso and reggae. The Mexican rock band, Mana, was popular, but it was everywhere, even in Chi. The Latinos listened to them a lot. Ken didn't speak much Spanish, but he liked the music. Marco Antonio Solis was popular, for the more romantic things, as was Vicente Fernandez. A lot of music in English. Bob Marley was a given, but the Eagles and, oddly, Mctalica, were very popular. Guns and Roses had a few that were played often.

Ken took all this in, in a subconscious way. He would remember it more exactly if there were a reason. It was a talent.

He soon went back inside to call the police station to say he'd be there in the morning to start work. A man who introduced himself as Donnie said they would expect him. They were a tight little group. He would be the first new cop in three years – if he made the grade, but population statistics said they needed another officer, so the city council had hired one.

The Chicago bit was mostly because Handy, their captain, Andrew O'Connel, was from there, eighteen years ago. He used the same methods, though, quite frankly, they weren't nearly that effective, here. It was a different culture. Keep an open mind about things until he learned the way things were done here. Expect the richer ones to think they could buy their way out of anything. It worked with the council, but not in Handy's department. Keep it that way.

"I'm just telling you this so you don't get off on the wrong foot with O'Connel. He's a bit hard to get along with until you know him. He's run four others off for the job you're trying for. He'll give you a rough assignment, to see if you've got the spine for police work. Complain, and you're out of here!

"This is a really great place. Hope you make the grade. Just want you to know it's not going to be easy, at first. Handy's impressed with a dedicated cop. Find a little something to do on your own, now and then, a little something extra that shows you're committed to enforcing the law, and he'll come around.

"Oh! He'll introduce himself as 'Handy.' Don't call him that until he starts calling you by your nickname. He wants to see if you respect his position. He doesn't really give a hot damn if you respect *him*. You'd damned well *better* respect his office!

"You can see I would like a new face here!"

"Thanks. I think we'll be friends. I've never been more than a hundred miles from Chi, before. I thought the pictures of places like this were phonied up in a studio. It's a trip to see there really are places like this!"

"Don't use that expression with Handy! 'Trip.' He's suspicious of anyone who uses expressions from the drug culture."

"Thanks. It's an expression everyone in Chi uses, now."

"You're staying at Wellwright? There's a place, The Leon's Den – Leon Lefevre owns it – where you can meet a cross-section of the people. It's on Divider Road, two blocks from the hotel."

"Divider Road? I guess anyone here will know where it is. What does it divide?"

"People. It's really Tenth Street. Your hotel's on Ninth Street. We call it Divider Road. You're in the upper city by one block."

"Thanks. I'll try it out. Restaurant?"

"Restaurant and bar and whatever. Food's better than average, and not too expensive."

"Whatever?"

"Looking for a date, sailor?"

"Hi, sailor. Whyn't juh come up 'n sue me sometime?"

Donnie laughed. "We'll get along! Got a call coming in. Ciao!"

Ken smiled at the phone as he hung up. He felt he really would get along with these people! He'd noted that they seemed friendly, even the ones who looked mean.

Well, he could use a good meal. Might as well get started and try out The Leon's Den!

Ken went into the station and to the desk by the door to say he was Ken Smart, there to start work.

"Nan Demarco. I'm sort of girl Friday – plus Saturday through Thursday. I sit here and try to cull out the real things from the 'I hate the damn bastard's guts and I'm going to cause him some of the grief he's caused me!'

"That's a clever way of saying we get a lot of complaints that are nothing more than personal gripes. There's not really much real trouble here. It's a cushy job.

"You really do look like your picture! The rest of the guys look like cops.

"I read your resume. Fred brought it over from the council building this morning. Your father and grandfather were cops in Chi. Handy – that's Captain! Sir! to you – might have known them. He's from Chicago. He'll be in at seven sharp. That's his hours, and he's strict about that. You were supposed to be here at seven thirty. It's five to seven. Believe it or not, that will impress him."

"I figured, if I'm to start work today, I'd better be here in time to get a little briefing."

"Day shift's too easy. He'll want to give you a night beat to see if you can handle it."

"Whatever. It will suit me.

"Will I be working with Donnie or somebody else?"

"You met Donnie?"

"On the phone."

"Probably not. You'll work with whoever's on the shift. There's one from one to four, two from four to midnight. Only one on the graveyard. That's the one that can be hairy as hell or boring as hell. Not much between. It's Monday, so things will be dull, usually. He'll probably put you on two. That's the more likely. Jose and Cal, today. We rotate shifts every second month. They can show you the routine. Mostly argumentative drunks and personality clashes. We haven't had a real crime in three days. We prefer it like that."

He said he'd grab a cup of coffee, somewhere. He could bring her something back?

"We have coffee. It's, contrary to cop legends, pretty good. I'd say to grab a cup, but ... you'll learn about Handy's little hangups. He might think you're being presumptuous to think you can drink our coffee before you're declared a working cop."

"I think I know the type. Very much down the line."

She nodded, and grinned. "Try Cathi's. They have really good hot coffee and pineapple Danish that are the best you ever tasted! One block left, and across."

He'd walked by the place, and had seen it was full. He said he'd try it. He'd be back at seven twenty five.

He walked in. Nan was talking with an officer she introduced as Cal North. She was right in saying he looked like a cop. Sort of bullish and crew cut. His uniform just missed fitting him. He had the traditional shiny black shoes. He seemed affable enough, and welcomed Ken. He said he hoped this one would make the grade. It was tiresome to get to know somebody for one or two shifts, then they were gone.

"They come, thinking it's a vacation job, all the way, and that they can lay around a lot. The place is run like a city. This is the closest thing to a city in three hundred miles. Handy's right by the book. You don't like it, the door out is the one you came in through. Don't let the knob hit you in the ass on your way out.

"He'll act sort of like an old pal. Get palsy on the job, and you don't have one anymore.

"Just warning you. He's ... he really is a pal, but only off duty. It's just him."

"I know people like that in Chi. Quite a few. It's because of IA, mostly."

"IA? Internal affairs? What's ... I don't get it!"

"Back about the time he left Chi, there was a big stink about cops getting into little groups of close friends and working shakedowns and so forth. A bunch of them ended up in their own jail. Even a suspicion got you into hot water and put a lot of pressure on you. A lot of innocent cops resigned, or left, because of the investigations. It's when IA got the reputation it has now. They got overzealous, and destroyed a lot of the good cops' reputations for a feeling of personal power, if what my father said was true. He was never investigated, but one of them threatened him with an investigation. He beat holy living shit out of the weasel, and said he now has a reason for investigation. There wasn't any investigation, and the IA shithead claimed his face looked like that because he fell down the stairs. They never messed with Pop again!"

"That might explain his attitude," Nan said. "It's the first time we've heard anything that might have caused it. He is a hell of a good cop."

A large man who also looked like a cop to Ken came in, asked if there was anything for him, Nan introduced Ken to O'Connel, who said to call him Handy, like everyone else. Come on in the office, and they'd see what they would see. It was nice that someone was on time, for a change!

"I was always taught to be prompt, Sir. I was told it wasn't something the people here would even understand, but I'm not about to change that!"

"I would advise that you pay very little or no attention to what people in other places say about this place. We run a tight operation. It's why there's very little crime, here. Being a police officer is a boring job, here. We want to keep it that way!"

"I certainly understand that, Sir! My father always said the best thing a cop can do is remove the reason for him being needed."

"Your father was a police officer?"

"Yes, Sir. Chicago, from eighty five to twenty ten. He retired with a clean record and excellent stats. He died in December of last year. He didn't like a life of not having anything to do, and, I'll always believe, willed himself to die.

Mom died four years ago, so he felt he'd already met all the obligations in his life."

"Which station?"

"Six for several years, then eight."

"I see. I worked both of them, one year at six, and one at eight. Worked four for a few months, but you know what happened there. A pile of shit, mostly, but a couple were dirty.

"You don't look like your father much, if I'm thinking of the right one. He was at eight when I came here. Not such a slender build, same hair. We used to call him Barney Miller. He looked a little like him."

"That was Pop! He and Grandpops taught me police work from when I was, as Grandpops said, just a squirt."

"Well, he managed not to get into the mess at four. Not a lot of us did."

"He had one confrontation, right from the first. He was out of it before they got crazy with it. He taught me to face that kind of thing at the first, not to hide from them. They wouldn't keep on, if you faced them down.

"Of course, if you had something to hide, you shouldn't be a cop, in the first place."

"It true how he threatened to kill anyone who investigated him? That how he got out of it? Had something on one of them?"

"No. He let them know his record was right there on the table. He was never around the dirty group at four. They could investigate him all they wanted, but they had sure as hell better not interfere with his job, and they sure as hell better have more than a suspicion without evidence. Police work demands proof and evidence. Until they had it, which they never would, leave him the hell alone!

"He was clean. He was the type who hated a dirty cop. He said all the good cops had to live with what a couple of dirty cops did."

"You can't know how true that is!

"Well, I don't doubt he taught you all there is to know about being a cop, so I won't bother with training you. I can put you right on a detail. You start tonight. Eleven to seven. It's usually quiet enough, but when anything comes up, it's not easy. You don't handle it, and I frankly think you're going to not handle anything much more than arresting a drunk, or that kind of thing, and you're out of here. I give you about a shift and a half. You stay on that shift for a month – if you're not out of here in a week."

Maybe this was only a test of some sort, but it seemed real. Handy did not like him, and wanted him to know it.

Why?

"Good enough, Sir! I'll spend the day walking the town. I want to familiarize with the layout and the kinds of people I'll be dealing with."

"You can use a cycle. You do ride a motorcycle, I assume. Your pop would have taught you that, at least."

"I'd rather walk it. You miss the details on a motorcycle or in a car. I'll want to meet some of the cast of characters. I'll want to know who's just acting. I meet them in civvies, and learn a lot more than if I'm in uniform."

"You would. Get Nan to give you a uniform. Never forget that you're a cop, and you're always on duty, uniform or no. Dismissed!"

He saluted, and went out. He was puzzled by the reaction he got, there. Nan asked how it went, and he said, "Very strangely." She gave him a uniform. It would fit.

Another was coming in as he was getting the uniform. Another one who looked like a cop. He was more Latino. His name was Jose Vincente. Nan said he was off shift tonight, that he would be on morning shift until further notice.

"According to Captain O'Connel, Sir! I should last a shift and a half," Ken said.

"Shit! What did you do that made him decide to get rid of you?" Jose asked.

"I don't have a clue. I may have something to do with my father, but I don't know what."

"Oh? Your father was a cop?" Nan asked. "Yes. That was on the resume.

"Damn! I should have warned you! He thinks you think you know more about being a cop than he does! He's funny that way."

"It is not funny!" Ken replied. "I'll have to show him I'm not that type, at all. I think there's something new to learn every day."

"First impressions are lasting, with him," Jose warned. "It took him four years to get over my coming back at him that Latinos aren't all alike anymore than Irishmen are all alike."

"Yeah. He resents it if you class him with the stereotypical Irishman in the movies, heavy drinker and total womanizer, then he stereotypes everyone he meets."

"Life in the slow lane," Ken said. "I'm going to walk around the town, today. I'll start near the airport, and work back uptown."

"They're mostly good people," Jose said. "There are a few who are bad news. Around the other end of the marina, there's a bunch of blacks who will probably try to intimidate you or rob you. Be careful!"

"Chi. I know a few little things. I wasn't on the streets, very much, but some of my best friends were. They taught me a thing or two my Pops would have gone ballistic about. Tommyrot was a Tae-kwan-do instructor. We would practice a lot of it. Crank was a street fighter, and really a hood, if I want to be honest about it. I know how to make a guy wish he'd never been born. He'll damned well wonder if he can ever have sex without screaming again. Angel, who we called Angela, was as beautiful a drag queen as you would ever meet, and as sadistic as anyone you would ever know. I saw him do some serious ass-kicking with three big rednecks, two ran away, and the other couldn't because he was laying on the floor, bleeding, and unconscious. Angela didn't have a hair out of place when it was over. He was royally pissed because he got a spot of blood on his gown, and broke a stiletto heel! He bought all us friend's a drinky-poo.

"I've been around."

"I'll bet you were popular with the queens," Jose said. "You're handsome and sexy. If you would, they'd like a romp with you."

"I've been there and done that, so long as it was on my end of the stick, only, but it isn't my thing. At all! It was sort of fun, a couple of times, but I just don't care for it."

"There are a few here. They'll like you, if you don't cut them down," Nan said. "Do *not* let

Handy know you'd even consider being seen in the same bar with them, unless you were called, and you had to be."

"Message delivered and understood. I got that impression. Chicago, twenty years ago. My Pops was like that, some. He tried to be fair, but you could see the disdain when a gay friend came over. He kept telling me never to be alone with them.

"I told him all I had to do was say, 'No!' It would end, then and there. He seemed to think they wouldn't take 'No' for an answer. I guess Angela could have raped me, or whatever, but I never did anything I didn't agree to.

"Well, I'll take this to the hotel, then walk the town! See you later!"

He went to the hotel. Maisie, at the desk, a big black woman with a happy attitude, greeted him warmly. He had talked with her for awhile when he went out last night, and liked her. She liked him. He wasn't uppity, like too many whites. She liked to laugh and make jokes. She said he was alright for a honky. He fired back that she seemed okay for a nigger. She cried, "Dissed! He called me a nigger!" He shot back that was true, she dissed him by calling him a honky! Turn about's fair play! She started it!

They became great pals, right then and there. Ken had that talent, and it was honest interaction. It was for fun, and they knew it.

He hoped he could be friends with a lot of the people downtown. He managed it in Chi, so he could manage it here. The people were a lot more open, here.

A thin accountant-type (there you go with the stereotypes!) came in, to have him sign some papers. He could take the receipt and copy to the station and he would be issued a uniform, shoes, and a gun. His name was Fred Wiley, and he would handle anything necessary with the council or other government agencies.

Ken didn't bother to tell him the sack he was carrying had all that stuff in it, already. He waved goodbye to Maisie, and took the things to his room. He then caught a taxi to the airport, and started his walk back toward uptown. He went up and down the side roads, learning how things were laid out, and where different things were.

Ken started at the place that was supposed to be the most dangerous, and the place where so much of what crime there was seemed to originate. A few of the men did seem threatening, but he just ignored them. There were plenty of "working girls" on the streets. He wondered where they found tricks. It would seem more likely that they would do better in the better sections.

After awhile, he saw. It was day, and a couple of cars with men in them would call to a girl and ask if she did housework. She would get in the car, and they would drive off. One was three Latinos in a car, and the other was a white man. He noted the cars and the license plate numbers. He would remember them for a few days, and could write them down, if he thought there might be a reason.

A very large and sinister-looking man with Rasta hair told him to give him five dollars. He said to go fuck yourself. The guy grabbed at him, and found himself laying on the sidewalk, with Ken's foot on his neck.

"Excuse me? You were saying?" Ken said, pleasantly.

The guy started swearing. Ken bounced his head on the sidewalk, lightly, and raised an eyebrow. There were several other people standing around.

"Okay. It didn't work," the man said. "No more shit."

Ken let him get up. "I'm Ken. I was just looking over the place. It reminds me of South Chi."

"They call me Rasta. You're fast, Man!"

"I've been around. A white doesn't last long in South Chi if he can't take care of himself."

"You can damned well take care of yourself, Man! Nobody had ever dumped me like that. A couple times, two or three dumped me, but it took awhile.

"I don't suppose you'd show me the move?"

"Moves. Why not?

"Okay, come at me like you did. Slow motion."

Rasta came toward him, and reached for him. Instead of backing off, he moved suddenly toward Rasta, put a foot behind his heel, and moved his elbow toward Rasta's face. Rasta went down. Hard. Ken caught his arm, and kept him from hitting the sidewalk again.

"Christ! I knew sorta what you would do, and it still worked!"

"There're a lot of that kind of moves. If I know you expect that, I'll use a different one – that I'm *not* going to show you!"

He laughed. "Man, you are cool!

"Hey, all! You just saw this skinny white dude dump my ass right! Maybe I ain't the bad-ass I thought I was!

"He picked me up and showed me how. He's my friend. Maybe he can dump me and can dump any of you, but I *know* I can dump any of you! Don't never forget that! I'm saying he's my friend, and you know how I am about my friends. Leave him alone!"

Ken said he could use a cup of coffee. Did any of the local places have any that was drinkable?

"Lita's is okay. I'm buying," Rasta said. He turned to a Latino man, and said Ken was his friend. This was Lucas Morales, known as Luke. He had the best ganja on the island. Good price, too! Just in case Ken was looking for a supplier.

"No. I don't use any of it. I like a beer, now and then, but that's about it."

They went into a little café, where a very sexy young black woman came to wait on them. Rasta introduced Lita Smith. A slender effeminate man came from the kitchen. Rasta introduced him as Cookie Hinson. He said he was called cookie before he became a cook. Another came in who was called Ned. Ned Marks.

They sat around a bit, chatting. Ken met ten or twelve other people, and got along well with them all. He finally said he had to get along. He was walking all over town to see where things were, and to meet people.

"You stayin' here?" Lita asked. "You ain't bad at all to look at. Might be fun in bed!"

"I'd give it my best shot!"

"You a rich Whitey, or gonna work?" she asked.

"Work. I'm the new cop on the beat."

There was a stunned silence. Luke suddenly laughed. "You for real? I tell you I'm dealing, then you tell me you're a cop? That's more than cool!"

"They told me not to pay any attention to ganja. If you deal anything else, what I don't know won't make me have to do anything."

"I don't believe me when I say you're the first cop I ever liked! You, I can trust, sure. You ain't bullshitting us," Rasta said. "I think you are a friend."

"But you wouldn't cut us any slack, we done nothin'," Lita said. "You gonna be the type what take the job serious-like, huh?"

He nodded. "That's easy! Don't do anything for me to have to cut you slack for that I ever hear about."

She laughed. "So we won't let you hear about nothin'! You still our friend.

"Y'know somthin' else? I ain't never called no Whitey 'friend' afore!"

Rasta walked a bit with him, and introduced him as his cop friend.

The section along the lower marina wasn't as bad a reputation. He talked with a lot of people, there. The guard at the marina, a man in his mid forties or so, chatted about the people who kept boats there. He was sort of in charge.

"Charlie Debbs. Born and raised near Billings, Montana. Picture me running a marina!

"Came here sixteen years ago to handle some business, and liked it. Never went back, never looked back."

"I guess you know about everybody here, by now."

"Hunh! Changes. About half of them been here more than six-eight years. Rich assholes uptown stay a couple of months a year, and run all over, the rest. What look like natives are from a lot of places. Some stay years, some only weeks.

"You gonna stay?"

"I hope to. I'm the new cop. If I can get by O'Connel, I'll be around."

"He's an odd'n. Probably pretty good, but he misses a lot of things, you ask me. He's by the book. Some people have read the book, 'n can work him. Gets bent if you try to tell him anything."

"You trying to tell me my job?" Ken said, indignantly.

"'Xactly!"

They chatted a bit, and Ken moved on. He wondered what Charlie was running from. It was just a feeling. He got it strongly while talking to a man called Mack Morton. He got it less from others. He thought this was an ideal place to disappear from somewhere else.

He soon crossed back into the uptown section. People weren't nearly so open or approachable, there. He got the feeling that more of them were running from something than in downtown. From listening to conversations, he figured it was mostly money things. The little hints were that there was a lot of "unreported" income here. Fiddle with taxes for a hundred grand, and buy a million dollar yacht, which was taxed for two hundred grand. There were a lot of snobs, there. He didn't think he was going to have many friends from uptown.

He ate a good meal, and went to the hotel to sack out at six. He would get five hours sleep, which was what he required, and would be to work ten minutes before shift. Handy would think more was to impress him. Ten minutes would be about right to actually do so. It was Sunday, the fourteenth of December. It should be a very slow night. Christmas wasn't a long way off. It was the lull between the early shoppers and the last minute shoppers. He would see the difference between night and day in the area.

When he went in, Yvonne Silva, the night desk clerk who got off duty at twelve, said he would just sit there, unless and until he got a call. The TV was out for repairs. It was, hopefully, going to be a long dull night.

"What happens if I'm out on a call and another one comes in?"

"It's a relay system. You throw this switch, and it transfers all calls to the hand unit, here. You always carry the hand unit when you leave the station."

"So I can patrol and have all calls come directly to me, wherever I am?"

She shrugged. "I guess, but why would you?"

"It's that or sit here with nothing whatever to do? I'd rather be out, talking to the night owls than sitting here, staring at the clock."

She shrugged again. "Up to you. Nothing says you *have* to be here.

"G'night." She left, as Jose and Donnie, who he met first time face-to-face then, came off shift. You didn't check out five minutes early. Ever. Donnie looked like a young cop, but was as friendly and open as he'd seemed on the phone.

Ken sat at the desk seat, and went through the drawers, then checked everything on the shelves and cabinets. He would know where everything was, and could put his hands on things quickly, when necessary.

He had a cup of coffee, and had to agree it was good. It was a very rich homemade mixture of Panamanian and Colombian coffee, half and half. Nan mixed it. Her brother lived in Panama, and sent the Café Duran. She bought the Colombian in the market.

An hour. One o'clock. He stretched, and picked up the hand unit, threw the switch, locked the drawers and cabinets, and put a sign on the desk saying to use the blue phone to call the black phone if he was needed in an emergency. He would return soon.

He went out into the street to walk around near downtown. Nothing happened, and there were no calls. He was at the desk when Nan came in, in the morning, with Cal, who was going on shift. He went to the hotel.

Ken went to work the ten minutes early. Handy was there, and asked how the night before had gone. He said it was quiet. No calls. He expected Yvonne to be there, not the captain!

"Oh! I forgot to tell them to tell you about tonight! I have to accept that it's my fault you're late!

"Listen, Smart. Tonight's one of the two nights everyone is here and on duty at ten. I thought they would tell you and ... no excuses! That's my job, and I didn't do it! I put myself on report for this."

"Sir! What's going on tonight?"

"Nobody reported anything. I can hope!

"There is a murder every fifteenth of December, and one the fifteenth of June. It's been going on for sixteen years. We haven't gotten one solid clue in that time!

"Those two nights, we all come on duty at ten. We stay on duty until twelve. I was in the marina area with Yvonne. Donnie and Cal are in the area just inside uptown, and Jose and Nancy are in the downtown section. I thought they had you doing the sweep detail, which means you stay very close to Divider Road, and move in and out of the sections, starting at the marina and ending at Front street, on the water, on the other side. You would take an hour going, and an hour coming back.

"I can't believe I didn't inform you!

"Okay. I reacted very badly toward you. I'm always hard on a new rookie. It's the only way to weed out the ones who would let us down in a critical situation. I still don't like you. I'll be honest with you, and you be honest with me, okay?"

"Yes, Sir. Might I ask why?"

"I was one of two people up for a promotion in Chi. Just before I came here. The other man got the promotion. We called him Barney Miller. I thought, then, and still do, that he started the rumor that made IA start investigating me right at that time.

"You didn't have anything to do with that. I'm human. I resent him through you."

"Sir, I swear to you that Pops didn't start any rumors, particularly with IA. He kicked hell out of the one who started on him is why they left him alone. They knew it wouldn't work, and he'd find them somewhere and do the same. He would never start a rumor about anyone. If he thought you were dirty, he'd be in your face in a heartbeat. If there were rumors then, I can find where they came from. It wasn't Pops."

Handy stared hard at him for a minute. "Do it! First thing in the morning!"

"Better now." Ken picked up the office phone, put it on speaker, and made a call to Chicago, to Millie Baskins, who was a very close friend of the family. She had been recording secretary for downtown, and all IA reports went through her. She was semi-retired, but did research work, when called. She was a genius with a computer, and had a linked station at her home.

"Millie? Ken Smart. I'm on a paradise island in the Caribbean, believe it or not! I hope to stay here. I need a favor?"

"Why, certainly, Kennie! Anything I can!"

"Back about twenty years ago, when that IA shit was going down so hard, there was a cop up for promotion. Pops was up for the same thing. Pops got the job. Director of patrol, I think.

"The reason Pops got that job was because the other cop had an IA investigation started, based on a rumor. At that time, that was a killer. Can you tell me where the rumor came from? Who?"

"Name?"

"Handy O'Connel."

"Andrew," Handy said.

"That's Andrew."

"Minute!"

There was a silence, for about forty seconds. "Here it is. A Connie Milton declared she saw O'Connel talking with somebody called "Tree" DeForest in an alley behind four. She said she thought DeForest gave O'Connel money. It didn't take long to learn that DeForest was an informer, and O'Connel was giving him money that was from the incidentals fund. Up and up. No Deals.

"Hmmm. Smart got the job solely because he had a lot of seniority over O'Connel. That was the only consideration by the commission. Their records were almost alike, except for that. It's part of the rules they have to follow. Equal merits always goes to seniority. Period. Case closed. O'Connel was a new man, and a good cop – and too young."

"Thanks, Millie. I love you!"

"You take care, Kennie. I love you , too."

They rang off.

"I'll be damned! I knew that, but was so pissed about the IA I never thought of it until she said that!

"Connie Milton. I haven't thought of her for years! I was dating her, a couple of times, but she wasn't right. I told her ... and IA gets a rumor. Bitch!"

Donnie and Cal came in, to report nothing had happened that they knew about. Maybe the killer had moved, or even died. They could hope. They chatted for a few minutes, then Jose and Nan came in to report there was nothing to report.

The phone rang. It was still on speaker, and Ken was on duty, so he said, "Smart. Police. Yes?"

"Officer, this is Sandra Carmichael. I live on North Marina Circle, number seven.

"Officer, there is something very wrong! Something terrible has happened across the street from here. Helena Vasquez has a little dog that yaps, sometimes, but it started about an hour ago, and hasn't stopped! She always shuts it up within a few minutes, but the thing sounds hysterical! I called her four times, and the line is always busy. The shades in the front window are drawn, and she didn't often do that! Something is wrong!"

"I'll be there in five minutes!"

"Oh, holy shit!" Handy cried. "I'm going with you!"

Donnie, Nan, Handy, and Ken ran for the car. Handy drove. They screeched to a stop in front of number four. They could hear the dog yapping in a frenzy in back. Ken ran around one side, and Donnie the other, as Nan and Handy went to the front door.

Ken raced around the corner, and saw a little fuzzy white dog scratching at the back door and yapping. He didn't wait, but yanked the door open. The little dog ran inside, and suddenly made a heart-rendering howl. Ken dodged into the kitchen to see a Latina woman, laying on the floor, by the sink. There was a small steak knife hilt sticking out of her throat.

Ken slipped on latex gloves, and told Donnie, who had come in a moment behind him, to open the front door for Handy and Nan. If he wasn't carrying gloves, use a handkerchief or something, and don't touch anything except the latch.

He took out his digital camera to start taking pictures of every inch of that kitchen, from every angle. Nan called the medical examiner. Ken said for nobody to go in the kitchen until the medical examiner came.

"Get the print kit and some gloves from the car, please," he said to Donnie. Nan said she'd get them. Ken looked at Handy.

"You're in charge. It's your beat. You seem to know what you're doing – so far," Handy said. Nan came in with two kits. Ken told her to print the front door, inside, and to print likely surfaces in the kitchen, away from the body. Donnie was to search the bedroom. Handy was to search the living room and bath. Put on the latex gloves before they touch anything. Use the camera in the car to photograph any least thing that might have anything to do with anything.

"No prints at all on the door handle!" Nan called. "We won't get anything there. Gloves."

Ken went to the back door. Same. Wiped clean.

Doctor Walters, the medical examiner, came in to be introduced. Ken showed him the body. He put on gloves and bags on his shoes. He noted, with a look, that none of the others there had covered their shoes.

Walters studied the scene, carefully, and asked if they had the sense to take photos. Ken said he'd covered every inch. He was printing everything. He hadn't yet found anything to take for DNA testing. Walters looked a little surprised, and bent to study the knife. He took out a small tape recorder.

"Almost an expert wound. Immediately fatal. She was stabbed, and dropped right here. There wasn't much bleeding, this time. The knife filled the wound and blocked. No apparent bruising. From the angle of the handle, I'd say she was struck at the base of the throat at a downward angle. There is no attempt visible that she made any defensive moves. It would appear she knew her killer. He – or she – was here, and had the knife ... there is water in the sink, and there are dishes and cutlery in the drain tray. Perhaps she was washing dishes while her killer was drying, or something. She turned slightly toward her killer, and was struck suddenly. She lived no more than a few seconds after that blow was struck. Her clothes are not in disarray. There is no evidence of rape or other assault." He looked at his watch. "It is one o'clock and three minutes AM. It is December sixteen, two thousand and twelve."

He took a small meter to pass across the body. "Ninety two point eight. The room temperature is eighty one point two degrees, Farenheit scale. Estimated time of death is ten forty to eleven ten, December fifteen, twenty twelve.

"Police officer Kenneth Smart will now take any prints he can locate from the immediate area. The knife handle has obviously been wiped, quite possibly with a dish towel laying on the floor (he took out a small ruler tape and measured) thirty seven centimeters to the right side of the body, as seen from watcher perspective. It is loosely folded, and lays seven centimeters from the cabinet base. I note a small amount of water under the left shoulder. Only a few drops. They may be significant.

"See photographs of body position and note that her left arm is folded under her body, which is laying on the back, and somewhat tilted to her left.

"Noted at time stated."

He dropped the recorder in his pocket, and asked Donnie to get the Gurney from the station wagon, and a body bag. "I'll removed the weapon at the lab. You can see it was wiped."

Nan and Ken stayed at the murder scene for another hour. Handy went across the street to get a statement from Sandra Carmichael. Donnie went with Walters to take the body to the hospital laboratory. They all met at the station to file statements, then went home at six thirty, except for Ken. It was, after all, his shift until seven.

He wondered if Handy was going to be on time. He knew Nan wasn't. It would be Cal's shift, but Handy told him to come in at noon, unless called at home, then everyone would be back on regular schedule.

Ken used the time until a little after his shift end to download his camera. He was going to study those pictures, very carefully.

He was also going to search the files for all the former killings. It seemed more than strange that nothing was found for sixteen years! He was damned sure he would have a permanent job if he could find something!

Ken came in two hours before his shift. He wanted to collect everything he could find from the files. If he was lucky, there wouldn't be any outside distractions, this shift.

The first thing to do would be to study the crimes. This was the sixteenth year, so it would be 1996. The files would be in the evidence room, which was a large closet with a lot of cardboard cartons in it in stacks. They had dates in marker on each one. They started in 1982. That was the time the town grew to a size where it needed a police station. They were stacked seven high, in five stacks. 2012-2 was on the top of a stack of four. 2012-1 was under it. 2011-3 was under that, and 2011-2 under that. The top of the stack to the left was 2011-1, with 2020-4, 2010-3, 2010-2, etc. It would be easy enough to find what he wanted. The bottom of the first stack was 1998-1. 2 was over that, and 3 over that.

He would start with 1996. He noted top box on the last stack on the other end was 1997-3. The stack to the left had 1996-1 on the bottom, with

2 and 3 above, and 1998-1, finishing that stack. It was all right there.

He dug out the 1996-1 box, and went through the files. Nothing. The 1996-2 box had a file, *murder unres: Betts* on the tag. That was the only murder besides *murder res: Carney by Flores: Dom* in the file. He assumed it meant Carney had been killed by Flores in a domestic argument.

The second was in the 1996-3 box. *murder unres: James.* He dug out the other files in an hour and a quarter of searching. He asked Yvonne where he could put them to study. She said right there. She was leaving. He put the thirty three folders on the desk, and took out a legal pad, then sat back to think.

He wanted a list of everyone who had been on the island sixteen years or more. That would take a bit of digging. It would be in the records. Everything was on computer, but he wasn't that good at retrieving things, though he did know the basics.

He wrote a list of the names on the files, in order, first

96-1 - Betts

96-2 - James

97-1 - Hendricks

97-2 - Lopez

98-1 - Little
98-2 - Thomas
99-1 - Vega
99-2 - Small
00-1 - Randolph
00-2 - Kitts
01-1 - Yerba
01-2 - Diamante
02-1 - Ho
02-2 - Samuels
03-1 - Williams
03-2 - Tantor
04-1 - Blees
04-2 - Zarias
05-1 - Kopek
05-2 - Wang
06-1 - Gentry
06-2 - Garcia
07-1 - Asther
07-2 - Fennel
08-1 - Florencia
08-2 - Gaynor
09-1 - Brian
09-2 - Roberts
10-1 - Dorado
10-2 - Kensington
11-1 - Batista
11-2 - Wang

12-1 - Governa
12-2 - Vasquez

Thirty four names. He separated the sheet into columns, and put details into their own column. First column was first name, second was age, third was race, fourth was method. He had found the big clue on that second column. Anyone, including a total idiot, would have had to see that from the first. Why hadn't they?

He now had:

96-1 - Betts	Arnold	27	w	k
96-2 - James	William	43	b	s
97-1 - Hendricks	Lucinda	29	m	s
97-2 - Lopez	Daniel	33	l	k
98-1 - Little	Elaine	35	w	s
98-2 - Thomas	Franklin	61	w	k
99-1 - Vega	Gloria	31	l	s
99-2 - Small	Henry	44	b	k
00-1 - Randolph	Ian	62	w	b
00-2 - Kitts	James	55	b	k
01-1 - Yerba	Kyle	22	w	k
01-2 - Diamante	Leon	24	m	b
02-1 - Ho	Mandy	37	o	s
02-2 - Samuels	Nathaniel	44	b	b
03-1 - Williams	Orisa	67	l	s
03-2 - Tantor	Paulo	22	l	k
04-1 - Blees	Quinten	22	l	s
04-2 - Zarias	Ralph	63	l	b

05-1 - Kopek	Stanley	76	w	b
05-2 - Wang	Tako	30	o	b
06-1 - Gentry	Ursula	24	w	s
06-2 - Garcia	Virgil	21	l	k
07-1 - Asther	Wesley	54	w	k
07-2 - Fennel	Xavier	19	w	b
08-1 - Florencia	Yvonne	41	w	s
08-2 - Gaynor	Zelda	78	b	s
09-1 - Brian	Aaron	26	l	s
09-2 - Roberts	Robert	62	b	k
10-1 - Dorado	Carlos	32	l	b
10-2 - Kensington	Darien	41	w	b
11-1 - Batista	Erika	20	l	k
11-2 - Wang	Freda	33	o	s
12-1 - Governa	Gala	27	l	s
12-2 - Vasquez	Helena	49	l	k

When you considered that William was often called Bill, and Lucinda was probably Cindy, it had to smack you like a two by four to the head! After that, it was more than obvious!

11 white, 6 black, 2 mixed, 12 latinos, 3 oriental.

They were all ages.

There were 12 females and 22 males.

11 were killed with a knife, 14 were strangled, 9 were killed with a blunt instrument.

34 bodies. All Ken knew for sure was that the next victim, if he couldn't solve this, would have a given name that started with "I."

They were in all sections of town.

He went back through. 27 were killed in their homes, 7 on the streets.

They didn't have nearly so many pictures at first as now, but there were pictures of the scenes. Ken went through them. Nothing stuck out.

Did it?

He remembered the Carmichael statement that the shades were drawn on the front windows. You could see in the house if they weren't drawn, if the lights were on.

You could see who was visiting, maybe?

He checked the pictures. The shades were drawn in several of the home killings. In all but one of the females' deaths, and that one was strangled on the street. In several of the males' houses, the shades were drawn, but in all the female cases, except that one that was in the alley behind the food market.

Ken wondered if the places where ... no. Not that percent of men were homosexuals ... but these were selected because of their names, so the ratio might not have any meaning, here. That would be held as an outside possibility. It would make these sex murders, possibly.

More than half the victims were married, or widows, or widowers.

Why would anyone go to so many houses where it wouldn't be seen as odd that the shades were drawn? That could be a clue!

The usual search was motive, opportunity, method. This didn't look like it needed a motive. It was a nutcase who pictured himself as being smarter than the police. He had left a blatant clue that had, apparently, gone unnoticed. The method was three different kinds of killings. The women were mostly strangled. A knife was secondary.

He went back through the files, quickly. The size of the victims determined knife or other. Larger types were knifed, smaller strangled, very large, blunt instrument. Opportunity ... was a puzzle.

There were voices out front. He looked up to see the sun was up, and Handy and Nan were coming to work. He was so engrossed he hadn't noticed the passage of time.

Handy looked at the files on the desk. "Learn anything?"

"In a way. Why the hell didn't you get word out about the initials?"

"We did. For the past eight years, we got the word out that people whose names started with a certain letter were to take the greatest care. They were to be with people they knew, or locked safely in their house, on a given night."

"Then I've learned that this guy is known and trusted by every one of his victims. He has to have been here for sixteen years. He thinks he's smarter than the police. He's probably fairly large, but is not as large as some of his victims. He would strangle more if he was that big.

"He is a guest in the houses of those he kills there. That could be because of profession, but it's iffy, because of the sparsity of his killings. Only twice a year indicates he would have time to set something up, so far as trust goes. It had to be someone they all knew. It was a man. He was visiting.

"It will definitely be someone who most people know. I'll spend this morning trying to find how many people have been here sixteen years or more."

"Not many of us, in the town. Downtown less than uptown. You can see some of the houses have been here a long time," Handy answered. "It might be one of those rich people who have become bored with life in such a tranquil place. It's, as you noted, a game."

Ken remembered something. A person who had been there for sixteen years, and a person that most people knew. A local character. He had an attitude that the police weren't too smart.

"What do you know about Charlie, the guy by the marina?" he asked.

"Charlie Debbs? He's just a local oddball. He's harmless. People like to stop by and gossip about the latest gossi ... My God! He fits, perfectly!" Nan replied.

"I think, before I go off duty, I want to see where he was last night, between ten and eleven thirty."

He put the stack of files in the box he had for that, and took them to the evidence room, then headed out the door. Handy was looking at him in a strange way. Nan seemed shocked, and had taken her seat at the desk.

Ken went directly to the marina. Charlie was sitting there, and greeted him.

"Hi! Didn't I see you by Brady's Bar about eleven thirty last night? Just outside?" he greeted.

"Might have seen me *in* it! I'm over there most nights, from whenever I leave here, and they close. Food's good and cheap. I like a couple of beers before I hit the sack. I only sleep five hours. My whole life."

"Yeah, I guess so. I looked in just before I went to the Velasquez murder scene. It was before it was reported, actually. I didn't know I was two blocks from a murder!"

"Heard about that. Sort of expected a killing, but didn't think it would be her. It didn't occur to me her name starts with 'H' or I would have warned her to lock up her place before dark, and don't let anybody in before daylight."

"You didn't know her name started with 'H'?"

"Spanish. They pronounce it 'Elena.' Silent 'H' in Spanish. I thought her name was Elena. Didn't dawn on me 'til I heard about it this morning."

"You know about the serial killings?"

"Hard to miss it, when the cops start telling everybody with an 'A' given name to stay with other people or lock themselves in, then six months later it's 'B' and six months later it's 'C.' Next day, a body. Don't need a genius to figure it. Been going on for at least eight – nine years."

"Or more. Try sixteen."

"Really? I guess so. You didn't connect until the police started telling people about the initial thing."

They chatted a bit. Charlie seemed to be smug about something, but that might be because of his regular attitude.

"You've been here for more than sixteen years. Who else?" Ken finally asked.

Charlie laughed. "You figured I'd tumbled to the bit about sixteen years, which makes me a suspect, huh?

"Let's see. The Donlevys, and Gina Corbell, but they're too old to be doing that kind of thing. Hank Burgess could be it. He's an arrogant asshole. Bill and Sally Baily. Carol and George ... they're even older than Gina. Doc Walters, but he was in school, sixteen years ago, in the states, I think. Morley Baines. Now that one, I wouldn't blink! Handy and Donnie, your police department. Yvonne, but she was gone away for more than a year, two years ago. Glenda Frome, head nurse at the hospital.

"Ask her! She's knows everybody, both sides of the tracks!"

"Thanks. I'll do that. You really were at the bar the whole night?"

"Yeah. Me and Phil and Jimmy and Ron were arguing about Obama and Romney. Some choice! The American people are being led blindly to the slaughter, again. I'm damned glad I ain't there anymore."

"There, I have to agree. You want the skunk or the polecat?"

"I'd be independent if I was there, and would vote for Paul, if he don't screw up before. He does pander to sorry pieces of shit, sometimes."

"Me too. See you later." He waved, and went on. He would follow Charlie's advice to ask Glenda Frome. That would be fastest. He would also check Charlie's alibi. It was too easy to make people who were a little drunk remember things an hour off, either way.

It would wait. He would go to the hospital, just after lunch. He would have lunch at Brady's Bar.

He did have one question. It was about those files, and who was at the scenes of all the semi-annual murders – or all but the first few.

Ken sat at the bar and ordered a roast beef sandwich and a beer. Brady was chatting with a girl at the end of the bar. He ran the place, himself, days, and had a bartender, at night. Sometimes he was around, sometimes not. He was personable, and got along with almost everybody. He had been there, according to the sign, since 1994.

He was the kind people would fail to say had been there that long. It wouldn't register. If Ken hadn't seen the sign, he wouldn't have thought of it.

Brady finally came over to greet and meet the new cop on the beat. He asked if there was any progress toward finding their local homicidal maniac.

"I have to go back to the first victim. I have to wonder if the killer did this someplace else, before here.

"You've been here for more than sixteen years. Did you know the first victim? Betts? Arnold Betts?"

"Arny? He was a bit of a prick, if I remember right. Attitude. Liked to get a little something on people and lord it over them. Like with that Johnson guy. Saw him with a local working girl, had a camera, kept hinting that Johnson's wife would get a kick out of that picture. That kind of thing."

"Johnson still here?"

"Nah. He went back to Texas in ninety nine."

"Bill James?"

"Didn't know him."

"Cindy Hendricks?"

"Called her Vavoom, mostly. Or Lucy. Only a couple of people ever called her Cindy. Semi-goodlooking. Pictured herself as a movie queen, and was willing to sleep her way to the top, if you get the drift. Had some kind of hangup about the local college boys. A couple of scandals, mostly because she was a mulatto, and those old families would go ballistic if their son was sleeping with a black."

"Local college boys? There's a college here?"

He laughed. "No. Local boys who went to the best schools in the states. Their families were the richer old ones. There were always four or five who we called local college boys. They'd come back here for spring break, or between semesters, or whatever."

Ken nodded. He asked if Brady had been there last night until closing. Brady looked shocked, then grinned. "I've been here for all of them. I'd have to be an idiot to think I wouldn't be looked at, from the get-go.

"Nope! I was with four people, at a private party, 'way uptown. Gina Corbell's place, on the hill. The Donlevys and Carl Krause were there."

"I wasn't asking because of you. Someone else told me he was here."

"I could probably tell you if they usually were here late. It's always the same ones, from about eleven thirty until two, when we close. I couldn't swear they were here last night, or night before."

Ken nodded. Brady had been on the suspect list for a whole five minutes!

Still, things were starting to add up.

He said he was going to the hospital to see Glenda. She would know a lot more about the people on the island long-term than anyone else.

"I have to agree. I hope you catch him."

Ken talked with a couple more people on the way to the small hospital/clinic that served the town. Rasta and Cookie were there. Lita had cut herself, and needed a couple of stitches. They chatted. Nobody they knew had been on the island for more than ten years, much less six-teen.

Lita came out, and hugged Ken. She said Cookie wasn't kidding when he said that knife was sharp! She had a bandage on her lower arm. They talked a minute, then those three left. A sour woman was there, and made a whiny complaint that she had been misdiagnosed again. She knew damned well she had cancer. Her mother died from the exact same thing!

"You told me last month your mother died of the same exact heart condition you had symptoms of, remember?" Glenda said. "Maybe you should find out what she did die of before you develop the exact same symptoms. It was hepatitis before that, right?

"Mrs. Stillwell, go home! We have people here with real serious problems."

"It's true! They say that guy on TV who says the government is trying to kill us all off is crazy, but here's the proof! Right here! You're trying to kill us off by refusing to treat the diseases you've engineered to kill us!"

"Which government is that?" Ken asked.

"What?"

"You said the government is trying to kill you. Which government?"

"Why, the fed, and all those."

"There isn't any fed, here. That's in the US. If they killed you all off, who would pay the taxes they're scheming so hard to get?"

"They want power!"

"Power over whom? If they kill you all off, who will their subjects be?"

"Go to hell!"

"See you there! Have a nice day!"

She stomped out. Glenda giggled. "Thanks. She's a pain in the ass. Every time there's a TV show about some weird disease, she gets it, and her mother died from it.

"You're the new policeman. Ken? I'm Glenda. What can I do for you?"

"Well, it's a real problem, because you doctors and nurses have a conspiracy to not find the cause of my death, but I know because my father died of the exact same thing!"

"Seeing I'm the one who's doing it, why come to me for relief? You aren't much of a cop!"

He laughed. "What I need is to know who's been on this island for sixteen years or more."

"About forty of us. I can eliminate several of us, because they're physically incapable of it, or are too old or sick. That leaves maybe twenty.

"It could be me, but I would be more efficient. I don't like to leave a mess for someone else to clean up.

"There's Sydney Ames. He's been here about eighteen years, and is a bit of a prig, at times. I think he's too prissy for the blunt instrument bit, and couldn't strangle a kitten.

"Dr. Walters said you've come up with strong evidence it's a man. I agree. He's a bit of an obsessive case with forensic science, and can take little things to make a big statement, as he puts it.

"He was here. Maybe the first couple of years he was away, at college, so that would let him off the hook, assuming he didn't take a special flight, just to do it.

"Handy was here. If this were a novel, he would be the one who did it to hide his evil past, or something.

"Daniel Saunders, at the marina. I think he'd definitely be noticed if he was around some of those peoples' house at night. He's six six, and weighs about three hundred twenty pounds.

"The marina. Charlie Debbs. I could picture it being him. He's a very strange psychology. He would be my first serious suspect.

"It would have to be someone who was here all the times. If he wasn't here for any of them, he's out. It would mean there are two, and have you thought about that possibility? Some knives, some strangulations?"

"Then two would know about it, and it would be out, long ago. Maybe five or six years, I'd be able to consider. Not sixteen."

"Hmm. Debbie Maxwell. She's as big as any of the men, and is a butch lesbian. Her, I could picture. I couldn't picture her killing the women, but you never know.

"John Fledgling. He could be here when we didn't know it. He lives on his fishing boat, and turns up in strange places.

"George Stanley. He could be, but I don't ... I can't picture any of the others, for a lot of reasons. We're about your serious suspect list. Nan tells me about it, and she said you would get to me, so I've been considering things."

"Brady?"

"Brady? Hmm. I never even thought about him. He's the type who's always there, somewhere in the background, never in your focus, isn't he? That's a natural defense mechanism for several psychological problems. Sociopaths are very good at it, usually. Like him, they're there, and seem normal enough. You don't think of them at critical times.

"I think he's the best possibility, so far! I hope not. I like him."

"I just asked to jog your memory. He has an airtight alibi."

Lucas Morales came in, and waved to Ken and Glenda. She paused, then said, "It could be someone over in downtown. We wouldn't be able to find anything about them – but I'd bet you could! I saw you with that Rasta character and his homo boyfriend. I'm afraid for Lita, at times. Rasta scares hell out of me, but he's always been nice enough to me."

"He's okay. He looks and acts scary so he won't have to *be* scary. He's basically a good person."

"He could literally break a person in half. Be careful around him!"

"Ken already dumped his ass, big time. He'll respect anyone who'll try, and Ken actually did it. They're friends. Ain't nobody downtown who would dare to give Ken any shit. More because they know damned well Rasta can dump any three of us, and Ken dumped him in two seconds. He even showed him how he did it! Everybody in downtown is practicing that one!"

"So it becomes a weapon everybody there has," Glenda said, giving Ken a look that said she knew just what he was doing.

"Well, I guess I have to consider that our killer is on that list," Ken said. "I'd better grab some shut-eye. I go on shift at midnight."

"In six months, you can have someone watching every one of the suspects," Glenda said.

"It's not going to be more than six days before I catch this one," Ken promised. "I think it'll all hinge on where three people were before they were gotten out of the way. The first victim is always the important one, in this kind of case. I doubt this killer killed a few to hide who he was actually after."

He went to the hotel, and had a good few hours of sleep, then ate a hearty late dinner, and was at the station at ten minutes to twelve. Yvonne said Dr. Walters had a report on the desk for him and Handy that might prove important. She went home.

Ken picked up the note.

Handy -

I found a bit of blood on the sleeve of the victim's dress on the arm under her. It is type B+ while hers is O-. It may not be of significance, but a person using a knife will often cut himself.

Hope this helps. How are things going? - W

Ken sighed. He didn't have any idea how many people had B+ blood, or if any of them were on his list, but didn't think it mattered much, except that it was found. He felt it did tell him something.

He read over a few of the files, then went to the computer, to bring up what he could about the first three victims and the people on the suspect list. First was Arnold:

Betts, Arnold George. Born Hanford Miss. July 6, 1969. Attended Loyola University 91-94. Medicine. Dropped out. Moved to Isla Verdante 95. Died May 15, 1996. Victim of murder.

Clear enough.

Williams, James Nathaniel. Born Macon Ga. Feb. 12, 1953. Moved Atlanta 1961. Bartender. Moved Houston, Tx 1972. Moved New Orleans 1988. Moved Isla Verdante 1993. Died Dec. 15, 1996, Isla Verdante. Murder victim.

It was adding up the way he figured, but hoped it wouldn't.

Hendricks, Lucinda Louise. Born Isla Verdante March 23, 1967, Died May 15, 1997. Murder victim.

Neutral in the equation, from that information. Now for the suspects.

Handy came in, and asked him about the paper from Walters. Yvonne told him about it, and he was on his way home from a party, so stopped. Ken handed it to him. He read it.

"Tell you anything?"

"Nothing I wanted to hear."

He saw the screen, and asked why.

"I think the killer killed at least the first two for a reason. The third might have been for a reason, or might not. He then noted that Arnold, followed by Bob left an interesting possibility. If Lucinda was called Cindy, it was something he could start a game with.

"Very few people called her Cindy, but a few did. Maybe he heard that, and started it, for the same reason. He now had A-B-C, and he liked killing. He liked thinking he was able to outsmart the police.

"As I said, the first two victims, at least, were for a specific reason. Any after those first two were for the initials thing. What set him off, and who he is, will come from knowing why he killed those two."

"I see. It's adding up.

"What next?"

"See what matches with my suspects."

"How many?"

"Six, I think. Including you."

Handy grinned. "Me?"

"You were here. You are in a position to hide evidence. I'd be a hell of a no-shower if I overlooked that little set of facts!"

"I still don't much like you. I do think you're probably going to be a good cop. I respect you. If you'd left me off that list, I would have held it against your record.

"What do you need to know about me? I'll be as honest as you are with me. So far, that's all the way!"

"You were here for the times I think are critical. Those first three victims were here, too. Were you ever in Macon, Georgia, New Orleans, Houston, or Hanfield?"

"Yes. I was in New Orleans in seventy four for Mardi Gras. Never in any of the other places."

"Then you're mostly out of it, unless something happened here between ninety five and when he was killed in ninety six. It's a fading possibility, but a possibility. You're still on the list, but 'way down."

"Good. I begin to think you might actually solve this one."

They discussed the blood. Ken said they had no way to attach that to the killing, or anything else. It would mean something, if one of their suspects was B+. Handy went home.

Charles Benson Debbs. He was a marine engineer, and a bit of a hippie. No record after leaving CalTech.

Sydney Allen Ames had been in Kingston, Jamaica, for three months, November to February, 1997. Out.

John Gerald Fledgling. In jail in St. Kitts May 5 – June 5, 1999. Assault. Out.

Daniel Drew Saunders. Possibility.

George Edward Stanley. In hospital Nov. 25 – December 18, 1994. Out.

He had Dr. Walters and Drew Stanley.

He brought up Dr. Benjamin Franklin Walters, just as the phone rang. A brawl in downtown, by the lower marina. He put the comp on standby, and took the car. He pulled up as Rasta and a big black man were circling each other. The man had a knife.

"Drop the knife, or I shoot you in the gut," Ken said, loudly, but in a calm voice. "I'm not in the mood for this shit, so I'd advise you to do as I say."

The man turned, saw Ken standing there, empty-handed. He calculated his chance before Ken could draw the sidearm, shrugged, and dropped the knife.

"Okay. What's the beef, other than you two trying to see who's most macho? I can tell you, it's Rasta. He was facing you empty-handed, and you needed a shiv.

"What else?"

"Fatso grabbed me and tried to feel me up," Lita said, stepping from the circle of people. "I'm his witness that it was in my defense."

"You got an answer?" Ken asked. The man had sidled close. He said, "Yeah!" and grabbed for Ken – and found himself staring up from the road at this cop with a foot on his neck.

"Fucking idiot!" Ken said, and bounced his head off the pavement. Medium hard.

"He wasn't around when you dumped me. I see the move works, if you're fast enough. I ain't. Yet. Good show!"

Ken looked at the hood, laying there, and sighed. He asked for the water bottle a girl had. She handed it to him, and he splashed a bit on the thug, then handed it back to the girl, who giggled. "You is cool, Whitey!"

The thug sat up. "Wha...?!"

"You've got one hour to be off this island, or I put you away for two years for assaulting this lady. Got it?"

He looked around at a wall of unfriendly faces. "Yeah. I got it."

"Come back, it's three years for being too stupid to go when you had the chance."

He stood shakily, and turned to go. Ken waved for them to let him through, and he went into the marina.

"He's got a boat. He'll go," Rasta said.

"He's not the type. He's stupid. Everybody get away from me.

"Rasta, get over by the gate, on the side where he can't see you, by those boxes."

Rasta nodded, and moved over. Lita grinned, and led the other fifty or so people away. Ken picked up the knife, and went to the car, as the thug ran out the gate with a pistol. Ken pointed to him. Rasta came up fast behind him. He tried to swing the pistol around, and suddenly found himself on the ground again, this time his head got a bounce that Ken feared would cause a skull fracture. He said so.

"Nah! His head's too hard to crack from that.

"What to do with him?"

Ken took the pistol, and went to the boat. He went aboard, and searched it for a couple of minutes. He gathered the knives and two other pistols and a rifle there were no bullets for, and a brick of cocaine. He put them in his car, then took a can of water to throw in the thug's face. When he sat up, Rasta snarled, "You got to be the stupidest one excuse for a stupid goddamned excuse I ever on this island! You don't learn, do you."

"Ungh!"

"I have the coke, and witnesses that I found it on that boat. I'll inform the coast guard about it. You have ten minutes to be clear of the harbor. Next time, I shoot you, whether it means I spend the rest of the night filling out forms, or not.

"Git!"

Rasta hauled him to his feet and bum's-rushed him onto the boat. He untied the boat, and threw the ropes onto the deck. The motor started in another minute, and the boat started for the open sea..

"He comin' back?" Rasta asked.

"No. I have all his guns and knives, and he's chicken shit without them.

"See you tomorrow!"

Rasta laughed, and waved. Ken went back to the station to turn the comp back on. It was hot, so someone had been using it. He thought he knew who.

He brought up the information. It was what he thought he'd find.

<u>*Dr. Dr. Give Me the News!*</u>

The screen came on. It wasn't the page he'd left. It was a message.

Ken and Handy –

Ken, you have my respect. You are far more intelligent than the rest of them. You only go by the book in those instances where that will work. I think you saw how I have been manipulating the evidence from the moment in that house when you noted the shades were drawn in a room where they seldom were. You said nothing, but I could see by your expression that you knew that wouldn't fit. It was the same in several others.

I will suppose you would wonder why so many would draw the shades and would consider, at least, that one might draw the shades if they were being examined by a doctor in the room with the best light. It also served to insure that others would not see me in the house.

Handy, you're a good policeman. You solve your cases rather well and rapidly. If I had not withheld certain crime scene evidence as the examining doctor you would have solved it long ago.

Ken, I executed my first victim because he was trying to blackmail me because of an incident that happened while I was attending university. He was a fool. He knew I would kill. That's all I'll say about it.

The second was because he was a bartender near the university and knew of another incident. He wanted to hold power over me more than obtain money.

I had noted already that the initials, A and B – we called him Bill – were a signal to start something that could be interesting. Life with no excitement or challenge suits many well, but I'm not among them. Life is far too easy here.

Lucinda was a girl I had some experience with. She knew my family would condemn me to know I had laid with a black woman. I was already starting down a road and I heard a man, her uncle or something, call her Cindy.

Bingo! My path was set and determined! A-B-C! I would garner excitement and exhibit my skill at puzzles! I was in a position where I could involve false data at times that would tend to leave me unsuspected. There was always the excitement that I would be discovered. You came and proved that was a reality I must face in a far more direct way than as only a possibility.

I knew as soon as I got back to my home that I had made a fatal mistake when I left the note about the blood on the sleeve. It proved to you that I have been manipulating evidence. I am in the position to put blood of any type on a sleeve. B+ is rare, here. Usual police procedure would demand that you start a search for all B+ donors. You saw it was planted evidence and ignored it. I think that, more than other things, focused your attention on myself.

I fear you will return soon and I must be away. I will have the excitement of knowing that I am running for my very life. I have the necessity of evading capture to survive.

I sincerely wish you well. It has been a game in which I was the master until you came along. Perhaps I will survive to start another exciting game, perhaps not. I wish to leave the game with a bit of class. I will concede with grace.

I confess to it all. I am yours truly, Benjamin Franklin Walters, MD. BFWmaster100@doc.blg

"Well! That rather says it all! Where will he go?" Handy asked. Ken had called him to come in to read the message.

"Does he have a boat?"

"Yes. And a plane." He called the airport. Walters had flown out four minutes ago.

"Do you have him on radar? Can you follow him?"

"No. We don't have the range. He headed north by northeast. Probably Cuba."

"Thanks. Can you have him intercepted, or can you notify anywhere he might land that he is a wanted escaped fugitive? A multi-murderer?"

"Yes. Will do."

"What do we do now?" Handy asked. "You've showed who's the best cop here!"

"No. I've shown how a fresh perspective can change things. I checked all those reports and files. Crime has steadily declined since you came here, to the point even the worst sections are relatively safe, now. When you came, a single cop would not have gone into downtown. There are about twenty percent more there now, and any of us can go there, without worrying about anything. You've got it to the point being a cop here is close to boring. That's the aim of a good cop. Make your own job redundant. That goal was something Pops always drummed into me.

"Something else he always harped on: If you have trouble with a particular job, hire someone who *is* good at it. *Who* does the job isn't important. It's important that the job gets done.

"I'm a damned good detective. I won't let go of that. You're a damned good administrator. The department isn't complete without both. I won't interfere with your job. All I ask is that you let me run with what I know about mine."

"Fair enough. I do have a damned good team. I've needed a detective. All I have are good beat cops. Now I have a detective.

"You're right saying I'm an administrator. I've accomplished some things here that others can be envious of. I've now got a detective, and good backup team.

"Now, detective! How do we get Walters back here?"

"We go to that blog and let him tell us where he's going. Do you really want to?"

"What?"

"He admitted to his first murder in the states. We have that in his statement. If they look for it, they'll find it. They can prosecute him for it, with the added information that he's an admitted serial killer. He'll get a death sentence as a result of the combination. This island won't have to pay for housing and feeding him for the rest of his life. There is no death penalty, here. We'll find him and let them handle it."

"If he's in Cuba, they won't get the chance."

"And he can never dare to leave Cuba. He'll be a known serial killer, and will be watched. He won't be able to stand that."

Handy thought for a minute, then shook Ken's hand. "It's four o'clock, and I have to be here in four hours. Hope it turns into a dull shift!" He left. Ken sat back and started figuring where a person of Walters' psychology would probably go. A slow grin moved across his face. He got on the computer with a message.

He then went to BFWmaster100 blog.

The blog was a lot of forensics scientists, and was mostly discussions of conventions and seminars and such. They did immediately put new science discoveries on the blog. Walters was the webmaster for the site.

Ken got off the plane in Nassau, and looked around. He had worked on Isla Verdante for only four months. The crime rate was down another couple of percent, which was partly Handy's policies, and partly the new open rapport with downtown. Rasta, Lita, and Cookie had started a gymnasium and community club for the youth. He was smart enough to be able to get through to them that, as he put it, "A life of phony macho games keeps cops and doctors employed, and is worth about a centavo to live. Get a skill or trade, and make it known that you're going to be the best damned person in that in the world – then do it!

"How many of you love the holy hell out of your parents, but get embarrassed when others are talking about what Dad or Mom accomplished? Is it because they wasted their lives? Because they never aimed for anything but the nearest cheap thrill, or bar, or line?

"This is a new world. It's new because *you're* here, now! Make that mean something! Don't let your tombstone read, 'He lived and died. So what?' Make it read, 'The world is better because he lived!' Make it read, 'Would that we all could walk in his shoes!'

"So you'll now say, 'Basketball and swimming and football don't accomplish anything.'

"Bullshit! Tell that to any one of the biggies almost everyone in the world will know the name of!

"So. Making money and getting famous would be nice, but how does that improve the world?

"It doesn't. It's just a big empty sack of shit. What does change the world is what you *do* with that money. *You* can make the world a better place!

"But not if you're going to stand on a street corner and act like a big macho piece of pig turd. Not if you're going to spend your life trying to get high. Not if you're going to try to have more sex than anyone else. Not if you're going to see how much you can shoplift. Not if you're going to be the toughest hood in the hood.

"Those are the roads to nowhere. Those are the roads that lead to your life being, 'So what?' Those are the roads to hell!

"I don't mean the church hell. That's more bullshit. I mean the hell you make yourself live in, right here!

"If you want to live like that, okay. It's your life. Just don't try to make me or anyone else live in it.

"Okay. Jim and Ponce will be defensive...."

Ken had been there. He was going to teach Tae-Kwon-Do and some police things. Nan and Yvonne were going to teach secretarial work and office procedures. Donnie was sports coordinator. Handy was business administration. Cal was marine skills.

It wasn't a college level thing, anywhere. It was basics, to try to find each individual's natural skills and abilities. It was the kind of thing Ken believed in. Rasta had turned out to be the same psychology. The cop and the hood were a lot more alike than a hood and a hood or a cop and a cop.

Ken smiled to himself. He fit. He never really did in Chi.

He went down the landing ramp to have a taxi take him to the Royal Caribbean hotel. He was attending a convention of forensics specialists. Some very well-known people would be speaking there, tonight. One, in particular, would be talking about CSI identification with limited laboratories. He was from Cuba, and had been noted on the internet for several very concise and accurate methods of identification of individuals.

Ken knew, deep inside, it was Walters. Too many things Dr. Llaves said on his blog matched too closely with what BFWmaster100 said on his.

Walters had flown to the Grand Banks, then had apparently taken a boat from there to Cuba. The plane was found on a beach on Grand Banks. The boat was the property of a person, William W. Williams, who spent only a week or less a year on the island. He had a small place there. The woman who was caretaker had a child, nine years old, who looked a little too much like Walters.

Llaves had been staying in an isolated place in the southern part of Cuba. Little was known about him, except that he was some kind of scientist. No one knew how much time he spent on his little farm. The family living there refused to discuss the doctor, as he was a very private person. He had the place there for nine years

It seemed as though Walters was prepared, for a long time, for this move.

Ken was seated to the far left of the speakers' table. Llaves was second from the far end of the table. They had finished the meal, and the meeting was called to order. Dr. Ana Veracruz gave an excellent talk on DNA preservation, and on the new techniques for decoding very small bits.

Dr. Nichols gave a short talk on identification of untraceable poisons.

Dr. Rommel gave a talk on ballistics.

Each had a short question and answer session. They gave such good instructions that there were very few.

Dr. Llaves gave a talk on detecting cosmetic changes. Ken stood for the questions. Llaves registered shock.

"Dr. Llaves, would you say that the cosmetic changes could best be detected through use of specific light frequencies?"

"Er, that is a major method."

"If I were to use a secondary ultraviolet source, would you suggest it would detect that your pigmentation is enhanced? That you are actually a fair-skinned person, not a Latino?"

"Quite possibly, if I had used a dye that was detectable with ultra-violet."

"Then more of a green light to show absorption by tannic acid dyes?

"The ultraviolet would show the fine scars from the surgery to change you nose, ears, and eyelids, of course."

"Yes, Ken, they would.

"Ladies and gentlemen, meet the best damned detective I've ever encountered, Kenneth Smart.

"Ken, what could you lecture this audience about that would fit into the detecting business and forensics?"

"Doc, I'd probably have to give you a very un-professional talk on modern computer tracing and educational aspects, in any field."

"That won't be necessary. You have already demonstrated the science, quite aptly.

"I will be returned to Isla Verdante?"

"No. Louisiana. They have your confession, and they also have the system and funds to prosecute."

"My confession? Really?"

"You confessed to a killing in Louisiana on the station computer, remember?"

He thought, then grinned. "Coises! Foiled again!

"Dr. Nichols, you are the world's expert on poisons. See if you can trace this one!" He picked up a shot glass that was beside his plate, and tossed it down, before anyone could stop him. He gasped, and pitched forward onto the table.

"Alcohol sodium carbonate extract of puffer fish toxin," Ken said, and walked out of the hall.

"... I want to know is how you knew the poison. Indications are that was it," Dr. Nichols said.

"He was studying that kind of thing on the web, three years ago, and eight years ago, and just after his last murder. I traced all of it. He didn't have time to erase the history, if he even knew how. He made a big mistake in his study of forensics to avoid studying computer science. Had he known, I would have played hell trying to prove anything.

"He believed he was the master. I think he liked chess. Some things on the net indicated that, but not as a serious player.

"You might say I was the unexpected pawn who took his queen. Checked. Concede."

"But why did you just walk out?" Ana asked.

"I was riding an ego trip, I guess. Here, I had trumped the professional. If I stayed, I would soon show I didn't know half of what I was parroting. I could look like my name. Smart!

"I accomplished what I set out to do."

"Yes," Nichols replied. "Capture the criminal, and see that he's prosecuted."

"No. I knew he was studying fast poisons. I'm practical. I couldn't see any reason someone would have to pay millions for support and courts and such for ten years. He was guilty, and had admitted it. He killed at least thirty five people. I could thwart what he really wanted, and did."

"You did?" from Ana.

"He wanted to be a famous serial killer, like Bundy and company. Now, he's a footnote in a forensics journal, somewhere. It's like a friend back home said. 'What do you want your tombstone to say? 'He lived and died, and so what?' or 'He made the world a better place.'

"He didn't suggest anything about him being a famous serial killer. Walters ends up with the 'So what?' epitaph."

"You're a real trip!" Ana cried.

"Don't say that around Handy," Ken shot back.

C. D. Moulton's works are available on most major outlets as printed or e-books. CD writes the CD Grimes, PI mysteries, the Det. Lt. Nick Storie mysteries, the Clint Faraday mysteries, the Flight of the Maita science fiction series, books on orchid culture and many others of many types. Mystery, adventure, intrigue, science fiction, fantasy, paranormal, mild erotica, and factual.